ROBERT WILLIAM PEARCE

ANTIBODY

ISBN 978-09556888-3-6

Copyright © Robert William Pearce 2010

OTHER BOOKS BY ROBERT WILLIAM PEARCE

ROBERT'S THEORIES AND IDEAS

Q.S. ALERT

BET FOR FUN AND WIN

Robert Pearce was born in Romford, Essex, U.K., in 1954. He was educated at Secondary Modern and Grammar Schools and then he studied civil engineering at Portsmouth Polytechnic and later gained an H.N.D. in building and a BSc. Degree in quantity surveying at the Anglia Polytechnic University. He has pursued many varying areas of employment including banking, dustman, dock worker, factory worker, electronic test equipment calibrator and window cleaning before becoming a quantity surveyor in the building industry. He retired from work at 50 because of ill health which gives him plenty of time for his hobbies and interests which are D.I.Y., woodwork, horse racing, oil painting, bird watching, chess, collecting British Victorian stamps and writing. He has lived in Colchester since the age of 14 where he now shares a flat with his wife Rose.

Dave Potts, a quantity surveyor in the building industry, is beaten about the head and dragged to the edge of the roof of a tall block of flats in an attempt to throw him over, only to be saved in the nick of time. He is an intelligent person who has a flare for theories and stumbles on one for a remedy for rheumatoid arthritis. Being essentially an accountant to the building game, it's not surprising he has confrontations with various people whose livelihoods depend on making money from contracts in a very competitive world. Despite this, he always conducts himself in a reasonable and fair manner and is generally a likeable person. So who would want to attempt to take his life?

CHAPTER 1

Dave Potts arrived as usual at 10am at Juniper House, a very large block of flats comprising of 52 dwellings in the London Borough of Southwark. He was the contractor's quantity surveyor on this contract, which was in the early stages. The scaffolding was up and some window replacement operatives were busy taking out the old Crittal metal windows in preparation for UPVC double glazing.

Dave was heading for the flat roof area, scaling the six flights by ladder. The tenants on the top floor had been complaining for several years on water ingress from the roof and he wanted to investigate at the client's request. Hopefully an instruction would then be raised for them to carry out the work which would give them an opportunity to make some money because there wouldn't be any competition.

He climbed over the parapet wall and started to walk across the roof when he was attacked from behind by two men. They didn't mess about, one swift strike to the head with a crow bar and he slumped to the floor unconscious. They dragged him to the parapet wall on the flank end of the block which didn't have any scaffolding with the intension of throwing him over the top. Just as they hoisted him onto the wall a loud voice hollered out.

'Hey, what are you bastards doing?'

It was Tim Brooks the site agent who had seen Dave arrive and wanted to know if he required any assistance. He was sprinting towards them screaming his head off. In an instant the two men looked at each other and one said.

'Get the hell out of here'

They left Dave with his head and shoulders dangling precariously over the edge and made a fast exit down the scaffolding and into an unmarked white transit van which sped away.

Tim didn't give chase; his priority was to heave Dave off the wall to a safe position then phone for an ambulance.

'Boy, you were so close.' Tim said as he phoned for the police; but he didn't get any response.

The ambulance arrived closely followed by the police. The paramedics carefully examined him to ensure there were no broken bones and it was safe for him to be moved. They then strapped him to the stretcher and hoisted him down the scaffolding to the ambulance, then off to hospital.

One of them said. 'He's going to wake up with one hell of a sore head.'
The other replied. 'Let's hope that's all he'll have.'

The patrol police, having spoken to Tim, quickly realised they were out of their depth and radioed for advice. Five minutes later Chief Inspector Blake arrived at the scene and realising this was an attempted murder, he instructed his officers to take all the operatives on site down to the station for questioning.

A team of six policemen scanned the rooftop looking for clues and came across a crow bar which was put in a plastic bag and labelled for forensic analysis. Unfortunately, nothing else was discovered.

Tim was the first to be questioned by the Chief Inspector at the station.
'What's your full name and address?'
Tim appropriately responded.
'Do you know the victim?'
'Yes, it's Dave Potts, our surveyor.'
'So you're an employee on this building site?'
'Yes, I am directly employed by G. Turner Builders as a site agent.'
'How long have you worked for them?'
'I've had that position for the past eight years.'

'What did you do before that?'

'I was on the tools as a carpenter; working self employed.'

'Are G. Turner Builders the main contractors on this job?'

'Yes.'

'Who are you carrying out these building works for?'

'Our client is The London Borough of Southwark.'

'Has G. Turner Builders done other works for Southwark?'

'We've done a few of jobs for them.'

'Have you worked on any of these previous contracts?'

'No, this is the first one I've been involved with.'

'Now, about Dave Potts, how would you describe him as a person?'

'Well he's good at his job, very thorough, a likeable person who gets on well with people. Basically he's a damn good bloke.'

'How long has he worked for G. Turner Builders?'

'Dave has been with the firm for about eight years.'

'Is he directly employed, or freelance?'

'He's on the cards with a contract of employment.'

'O.K., please now describe what happened?'

'Well, I saw Dave arrive on site at about ten-o-clock, that's the time he usually arrives most days for about an hour or so. I was dealing with a couple of subcontractors at the time. He was making his way up the building and I followed, although he wasn't aware of my presence. I reached the roof and there were two men dragging him over to the edge. So I shouted and ran towards them at which point they dropped him and ran off. I couldn't give chase because he was hanging dangerously over the parapet wall. My main concern was to pull him back. By the time I'd done this the two men had made there escape down the scaffolding on the flank end. I then rang for the services.'
'Can you give a description of the two men?'
'They were both white in their late twenties. One had a shaven head, was very well built and well over six feet tall. The other had black wavy hair of average build and height. I think I would recognise them if I saw them again'
'What were they wearing?'
'The big fellow wore a white short sleeved T-shirt, blue denims and black shoes. The other chap was wearing a green long sleeved T-shirt, black denims and shoes.'
'Did they say anything?'
'Something very brief was said by one of the men, but I couldn't hear what.'

'Could you make out any accent?'
'No, they were about fifteen or twenty metres away and it sounded like an abrupt statement spoken quietly?'
'Can you think of any reason or anybody who would want to harm Mr. Potts?'
Tim hesitated, which the inspector noted.
'No, not really.'
'Not really isn't a conclusive answer!'
'Well he's a likeable chap, but being in his position essentially controlling the money, it's difficult to keep everybody happy all the time.'
'Please continue.'
'You see I've heard things said, but nothing really threatening, not as far as I'm aware anyway.'
'What sorts of things have been said?'
'For example occasionally a subcontractor might get a bit uptight if he's not paid what he thinks he should be paid, or his payments have been delayed for one reason or other, like the Dave hasn't been paid by the client, or there are contentious issues still to be resolved. Those sort of occurances. But that's all part and parcel of the job'
'O.K., thanks very much for your help Mr. Brooks that will be all for now.'
Tim slowly rose from his chair and left the station, but he knew he would be back.

CHAPTER 2

Dave Potts was a contractor's quantity surveyor for G. Turner Builders. He was in his late forties and had a wealth of experience. Dave had numerous qualifications having studied civil engineering and electronics before entering the building industry as a quantity surveyor. By any stretch of the imagination he was not a high flyer at school but had developed a very good level of intelligence and an active mind by working hard and learning a broad spectrum of academic skills.

His father was an intelligent person, who like his two brothers, had had a private education which was quite a rarity in the late 1930's and early 1940's. The family weren't extremely wealthy but were quite comfortably off, having come from a long line of insurance employees, which at the time was a very well paid occupation.

His father had served in the R.A.F. for his National Service, then continued for a further four years; he had a love for flying. He was a radiographer in the R.A.F. having been grounded which is where he met his wife who was a nurse. He later became an insurance agent like his forefathers, but didn't want Dave to continue the family trend because he enjoyed his social life and the majority of this work was carried out in the evenings.

His mother came from a family of builders, her two brothers being carpenters. Her grandfather went to Canada with his wife and son and worked on the huge dam by Niagara Falls. He later told stories of how lucky he was not to fall into the concrete being laid which is how some poor men met their end. He also was a head ganger in moving houses which was done at night when there was nobody else around. The Canadian houses were made of timber and had no foundations, they were simply jacked up and put on tree trunks and rolled along-quite amazing really.

His wife also made a lot of money in having a shop. She managed to get a loan to start her off and it took off from there. They came back to England having made their fortune and he retired at thirty. In fact he never had a proper job at all; he was a wheeler and dealer, never qualifying for a state pension because he hadn't paid any National Insurance Contributions. He dabbled in property and built a lot of houses and flats which he rented out.

Being a relatively quiet sensitive person Dave avoided confrontations where possible, but enjoyed the company of others carefully avoiding being the centre of attention. He enjoyed his home life with his wife and had many interests like bird watching, playing computerised chess, D.I.Y. and philately, to name a few. He was not a materialistic person, disliked expensive fast cars and avoided getting into the 'keeping up with the Jones's' syndrome.

He had suffered from chronic rheumatoid arthritis (R.A.) for twenty five years and was currently taking steroids and anti-inflammatory medication. About ten years ago he was having gold injections which worked well for a few years, but he had to come off them because he developed erratic heavy rashes, a known side effect. His mates joked that he had the most expensive bum this side of the Watford Gap, a frequent comment which he didn't mind, taking it in his stride.

Methotrexate was then taken for a couple of years which he didn't respond to; in fact it made his mobility worse, which is unusual. Also, this was very difficult to get off, but he managed it with determination. Pain killers were not taken, unless he had a flare up of inflammation in his knees, then it was only paracetemol. It was Dave's belief that God didn't want him to suffer any more and consequently had taken away his pain.

The progress of his condition had simmered down for several years and appeared to be more dominant when he was stressed. The weather and what he ate had little affect, contrary to popular beliefs. His wife had introduced him to a high strength Glucocamine Sulphate, taken daily in tablet form which after a couple of months made a marked difference reducing stiffness, particularly in the morning when he got out of bed. She was advised by a friend whose husband had taken it and was able to ride his bike again. In fact they were so pleased they have started giving it to their dog, to which Dave's amusing comment was 'I suppose he's riding a bloody bike as well'.

As a consequence of his active mind, he had an inspirational thought for a remedy for R.A; it was his belief that the condition could not be cured. It is well known that the cause of this complaint is an antibody in the blood attacking good tissues in the joints causing them to inflame. What causes this occurrence has been closely looked at for years, unfortunately without a solution.

Now, the purpose of antibodies is to attack foreign unwanted matter and different antibodies attack varying toxins. Dave thought that if all the toxins known to man were introduced individually, then one could determine which antibody reacts to which toxin. Hopefully, it could then be established which foreign body the harmful antibody would normally work on. If this was then given to the patient, then the antibody would act on it rather than attacking the good joint tissues; in effect giving it something else to do.

Dave emailed his theory to the Arthritis Research Council, only to get a rude blunt reply stating they currently spend hundreds of thousands of pounds a year in research engaging highly qualified scientists whose approach was from basic medical sources. He was further advised to let them carry on with their good work and that he should concentrate on his usual day to day duties.

On receipt of this reply, Dave was initially disappointed, but after careful thought he became excited. He'd obviously rattled a few cages. Maybe they wished they'd thought of the idea first? Perhaps they were already working on something similar?

He made contact with his G.P., who thought the theory was very innovative and was amused by the response he had had. His consultant rheumatologist was equally interested, stating that he had read a medical research report where they had been working on similar lines, which would explain the abrupt rude response he received.

So he decided to write to the British Medical Association. Their initial response was far more encouraging. They then held a meeting in London to discus the theory. Several eminent doctorates of medicine and Dave were present. They concluded that it was indeed a big breakthrough although they were conservative about the time it would take to develop the idea.

Two days later a press conference was called and it made headline news in the papers the following morning. It was also the main T.V. news report and Dave was inundated for requests for interviews with journalists. He took a fortnight off work to conduct these duties and then a further week to chill out. The pressures were immense, everybody wanted to talk to him; the phone didn't stop ringing.

Dave was over the moon. He'd had many bright ideas in the past, some of which proved fruitful, but nothing like this. It appeared that overnight everybody wanted to be his friend, people completely unknown to him would stop and chat and shake his hand. It was a great feeling and he was thoroughly enjoying it.

About three years previously he had written to the Civil Aviation Authority with his first theory on jet lag, but had not received a particularly favourable response. Being keen on birds, he was aware that when they migrate they use the earth's magnetic field as a guide. This had been proven by placing small magnets on the side of their heads to deflect the field. As a consequence they flew in different directions, not knowing where to go. So he surmised that they must have sensed some form of energy, birds being very sensitive creatures.

Humans, being far less sensitive, are not able to navigate using this method, but nevertheless do receive some form of energy when crossing the earth's magnetic field. Because this field goes from pole to pole, it is far more noticeable when travelling by aircraft from east to west, or west to east, because you are cutting through the field. Now from Dave's school days having studied physics, he was aware that if you pass a body through a magnetic field it produces an electrical current. This is the energy produced. Consequently, although passengers are not aware, a form of energy is induced which causes the sensation of tiredness, commonly known as jetlag.

He suggested that a solution to this phenomenon would be for the passengers to wear some form of headgear containing magnets to deflect the field. Perhaps a more practical solution would be an analogy of ships having an electrical current running around its outside to prevent corrosion. An electrical current passed around the shell of an aircraft would deflect the earth's magnetic field consequently solving the problem. This was Dave's first and favourite theory.

Another theory, which the Civil Aviation Authority wrote back to say they were 'extremely interested in his observations', was to prevent blood clotting on long haul flights. This was a hot potato hitting headline news several years ago.

Being an arthritis sufferer, Dave was fully aware of various comforts for his complaint. One of them was the height of chairs. He noted that it was far more comfortable to sit with the level of your buttocks above that of your knee. In effect, if your knee level is higher then the heart has to pump the blood uphill, so to speak, which is far more difficult. If remaining in this position for lengthy periods of time it puts a strain on the system causing clotting. So raised seating and occasional exercise was recommended.

He had other ideas as well which would no doubt come to light in future interviews with the press for newspaper and magazine articles.

CHAPTER 3

George Turner formed his company G. Turner Builders in the early 1980's having been a sole trader as a carpenter for many years. He started in the building industry the day he left school. His father, who was a milkman, recognised his skills and aptitude to woodwork at an early age and had a friend who was a local builder. So he took George along to see him and he agreed to take him on as an apprentice for four years. During his training he also attended night school which proved to be very beneficial.

He gained a lot of experience with this builder and was employed, like the majority of carpenters at the time, on the cards. As time progressed being self employed became more fashionable and it generally paid more providing you could maintain a steady flow of work, so George handed in his notice and became self employed. But it was not all plain sailing; the building industry is notorious for booms and slumps. Being the major employer of people in the U.K. it is used by successive Governments as an economic regulator. Consequently, when the country goes into recession building stops almost overnight and you can't get a job for love or money.

George still kept in contact with the builder who gave him his first job, quite often carrying out work for him. Then in 1982 the builder decided to retire and gave George the opportunity of taking over the business which he accepted.

The organisation had a main office which employed a full time secretary, an estimator who also served as a quantity surveyor who was nearing retirement and a young assistant. There was also a reasonably sized yard with storage containers.

They specialised in the refurbishment of existing buildings and carried out a lot of work for The London Borough of Southwark. They also had private clients like banks and building societies, but very rarely engaged in new build projects.

George liked working for local authorities; they were his bread and butter. They didn't necessarily pay the most money, but at least it was guaranteed, unlike some of his clients in the private sector who wouldn't pay up for one reason or other. There was also the added advantage that they had a yearly spend budget which didn't fluctuate too much which ensured a steady flow of profitable work, which is the prime objective of any successful company. Furthermore, their work was an absolute necessity in recessionary periods when private work dries up.

When their estimator/surveyor retired George poached Dave Potts from Southwark Building to come and work for him. It came at a convenient time for Dave because he was growing more and more dissatisfied with his current freelance work and George offered a far more attractive and secure position. Furthermore, with Dave's contacts within Southwark Building it opened a lot more doors for George.

CHAPTER 4

The London Borough of Southwark is the second largest London Borough, Lambeth being the biggest. It covers a very large area in the south east of London and is extremely densely populated. During the 1950's and 60's architects were given a brief of providing housing for a given amount of families and individuals within a predetermined area of land.

As a consequence of this large blocks of flats were built. It was the only way they could accommodate such a volume of people. Being so cramped together, this unavoidable housing strategy has caused some social problems, but not as much as you would imagine. Many of the residence have very similar backgrounds and have known each other a long time. In fact it's fair to say that throughout the Borough there is generally good neighbourly conduct.

There are obviously exceptions to this but being in London there are ample opportunities to find work other than in recessionary periods. Having a disposable income goes a long way in improving their quality of life and statistically has the knock on effect of reducing crime and street violence.

Regarding council housing, Southwark is split into nineteen different neighbourhoods, each having its own office where teams of housing officers carry out administrative roles just like other Boroughs throughout the country.

There are a lot of people residing in Southwark who have varying cultural origins, particularly Nigerian. Consequently, there are many public sector employees of varying ethnic backgrounds and my experience is that most of the time they all seem to get on very well with each other, which is good.

Southwark Building and Design Services, as it was named in the late 1990's, are assigned by the various neighbourhoods to draw up bills of quantities and specifications for carrying out necessary building, refurbishment and maintenance works of a reasonably large scale. They are based at Spa Road. The day to day general small scale maintenance works is done by a contractor who had submitted the successful tender of the term building maintenance contract, which usually lasts for three years.

The larger scale or more commonly termed major works are in excess of £10K-£20K and frequently amount to hundreds of thousands of pounds. They are generally of a cyclical nature, occurring every five to ten years, particularly the external redecoration of blocks of flats. There are also programs for the installation of UPVC windows and doors replacing the existing which are timber or metal. Re-roofing is another maintenance job. Concrete repairs are also written into the contracts. Asbestos removal by specialist subcontractors is also included. Public buildings and schools with concrete in their structure frequently have these surfaces chemically cleaned.

So there are several elements to be considered when maintaining a building. Consequently, the architects and surveyors employed are required to be suitably qualified. A clerk of the works is frequently employed as the architect's representative on site to ensure the work is carried out to the correct specification.

All of the maintenance term contracts used to be carried out by a Southwark building unit which was based at Frensham Street. They employed direct labour on the cards; none of them were of a subcontract nature. During the late 1980's the Government decided that all such public organisations should be financially accountable and competitive with the private sector. In other words to survive they had to show a profit or else they would be closed down.

So each neighbourhood's maintenance term contract was put out to tender and outside contractors were invited to submit their prices. As time progressed the Southwark building gradually lost some of the contracts to the private sector. Occasionally they would win back some of the contracts for the period and initially the competition was fierce.

In hindsight, a general observation was made that the Southwark building unit provided a better service because customer satisfaction was very high on their agenda, whereas the top priority of private sector builders was to make money. But as time progressed, in order to survive, making money was the ultimate aim for both the public and private sector organisations. Consequently, unfortunately it has to be said that although money was arguably saved, it was at the expense of the quality of the end product.

Furthermore, the Southwark building unit arguably provided better value for money. Private organisations initially found it difficult to enter this market, but they became shrewd and forwarded very low tenders, some of them at cost with very little or no profit margins. It was really a combined effort to try and push the Southwark building unit out of the market, which is what eventually happened, they lost a lot of contracts, then had to make their workers redundant and consequently over the years gradually diminished in size until eventually they were shut down, which is a great shame because they provided a very good service.

Fortunately for Southwark's direct labour team, a system was set up whereby they could transfer over and be directly employed for the new private sector building company who had won the tender and been awarded the new term contract.

The strategy by the private sector of submitting low tenders at cost was crafty because once they got their foot in the door having successfully got the Southwark building unit out of the way they then pushed up their tender prices. So the Governments bright idea of trying to save money was very naïve and foolish because the relatively low public sector tenders dampened down the price and they were very well organised and did a far better job at a reasonable price.

Southwark Borough Council also had its own section for larger scale works initially called Southwark Major Works which was based at Debnams Road. They had one contracts manager, two quantity surveyors, two estimators and four site agents who were directly employed. The surveyors and site agents had worked for Southwark for a number of years, whereas the contracts manager was taken on when the unit was set up in the early 1990's.

The contract manager's job was to run the set up, which was a very difficult job and their employment didn't last very long mainly because they had disagreements with the senior building management team at the head office in Frensham Street.

Southwark didn't want to make the commitment of employing staff on the cards with employment contracts with all of their benefits, so they took on staff through agencies with only one week notice either way and no holiday or sick pay. Several quantity surveyors and site agents were working under these conditions alongside staff that enjoyed better pay and all the benefits of a full time position with a contract of employment. Dave Potts was one of these agency quantity surveyors before he left to work for G. Turner Builders.

Furthermore, there was a fiddle going on between the managers of the building unit and the agency which ironically supplied the majority of the agency workers. They were pocketing a pound or so for every hour they worked, payday was at Christmas time. This angered Dave Potts when he found out and greatly contributed to his decision to leave.

In order to substantiate their existence under Government legislation the Major Works building unit had to make a profit which they did quite comfortably for a number of years. Then the big crunch came. A huge contract in excess of £10M was put out to tender, it was called Browning, the name of the estate in Southwark where the works were to be carried out.

The works were to be carried out on several large blocks of flats and was being financed by the Government in what was called a Capital Initiative Scheme to improve the homes of the occupants to fall in line with a Decent Homes to Live In proposal, also set up from public spending by the Government nationally.

It included installing new lifts, replacing windows and doors, re-roofing, concrete repairs, painting and decorating, and internal works like replacing the heating system and installing new bathrooms and kitchens. So the works were very extensive and the contract period was three years.

Senior Southwark building management were very keen to win this contract for political reasons. So they worked hard in putting together a tender, but the chief estimator was not experienced in contracts of this scale, in fact neither were the building management. They were treading on dangerous grounds.

When it came to the adjudication stage, which is when the management have a meeting to discuss their proposed tender submission, apparently several issues were addressed, including the fact that they had not priced anything for head office accommodation because this was obviously a public building which was rent free. Whereas private contractors would have had to price this item to because they didn't have the same benefit and would incur a cost. Furthermore, it is at this final stage that the management decide whether add a price to the tender to hopefully increase their profit margins, remembering that to be successful their tender must be the lowest.

Apparently there were mixed opinions whether to add to the tender sum, but the senior building manager failed to listen to the wise advice of his delegates, he was thinking only of himself and was keen to win this prestigious contract at all costs foolishly only seeing that it would look very good for his career prospects. But as it happened it turned completely against him because they submitted a tender of £10M and won the contract by £2M, which was the difference between them and the next lowest tender.

It was clearly apparent that Southwark had made a mess of the tender because it was far too low judging by the market. This was primarily because they were all grossly inexperienced in dealing with a contract of this size. In fact nobody had been involved with a contract in excess of a few hundred thousand pounds before.

Dave Potts had a confrontation with the head estimator basically saying that he hadn't done his job properly and that he must have known he was out of his depth and asked for help by suggesting to senior management that they engage a suitably qualified estimator. But he was probably worried about his position if he admitted that this tender was really beyond his capabilities.

Now in a situation like this in any contract the construction organisation with the lowest tender is given the opportunity to stand by his tender or withdraw. Under normal circumstances because the margin between the lowest and next highest tender was so large, they would have withdrawn. If they didn't, then almost certainly the client's quantity surveyor would not have awarded them the contract anyway because they knew the contractor would not be able to carry out the work for that price and run into financial difficulties during the contract period and have to pull out which would mean that another contractor would have to be engaged to complete the works at some considerable expense. Furthermore, nobody wants to see a contractor going to the wall unnecessarily.

But this was no ordinary situation. The client and the builder with the successful tender were both of the London Borough of Southwark Empire. Serious meetings took place between the client, which was the Borough Neighbourhood and Southwark Building management. It was concluded that although Southwark Building would make a loss, it was cheaper for Southwark Council as a whole if they did the work rather than pay £2M more engaging an outside contractor. Plus the fact it was a very prestigious contract. Unfortunately, because of Government legislation, Southwark Building has to make a profit, which it wouldn't do after the three year contract period was up, so the building unit would be closed down and all the staff would loose their jobs.

A separate building unit was set up for this contract with the assistant head quantity surveyor at Frensham Street managing it. He quickly realised that it would end in disaster so he formulated a plan.

He approached the Director of Building at Spa Road and put a proposal to him. This was to combine the successful Major Works building unit with the new Browning unit, with him managing the whole outfit, pushing out the existing Major Works manager.

He incorrectly forecast the combination would be a success with the profits of Major Works offsetting the losses of Browning and the foolish Director bought it, although it had been said by a few 'in the know' that he wanted as much of the building sections closed down before his retirement, which was approaching, to cover up his dodgy goings on, so really this new set up suited him down to the ground.

Indeed, that's what happened, he took over as the manager for three years and then the whole building unit was closed down when they made their inevitable loss. It was during the earlier part of this period that Dave Potts left to join G. Turner Builders.

CHAPTER 5

It was common knowledge that Simon Ratcliff, a senior quantity surveyor for The London Borough of Southwark, was as bent as a nine bob note. If you wanted to win a contract at an inflated price, then he was the man to see. Simon was tall and slim and in his early fifties. It was a source of amusement throughout the building circle how on earth he managed to keep an attractive blond in tow as his bit on the side being married with four children, because he had a face like a bag of spanners. Money was probably the motive and he had plenty of it to throw around. His salary was in excess of £45,000, but that was small meat to his underhand benefits.

Nobody liked him, he was arrogant and bad tempered, in fact it's difficult to imagine how he'd reached so high up the ladder; that is to those who were unaware of his personal life because rumour had it he was having a ding dong with the Director of Building, another ruthless character who gained his position through nepotism.

George Turner, the managing director of G. Turner Builders, had been on Southwark Council's approved list of contractors for several years, having invested large sums of money to satisfy the necessary criteria. He recently had to increase his public liability insurance from £1.5M to £5M, restructure his entire organisation to meet the requirements for a quality control BS5750 certificate and then there was Simon's brown envelope up front with the agreement of 5% on all future contracts.

George had recently completed two contracts, was half way through a one and had just started another, but things weren't working out too well. He had just broken about even on the most recently completed contract, despite favourable agreements on extra works and day works (a lucrative method of payment in building contracts whereby the contractor submits a standard sheet of paper with the number of hours taken for items of work not in the bill of quantities which is a pre contract document with all the items of work measured by the clients quantity surveyor from drawings and information supplied by the architect. The bill of quantities is essentially a tender document for all invited contractors to price; the best price winning, which is usually the lowest).

All daywork sheets are signed by the clerk of the works (the architects representative on site to ensure the work is carried out in accordance with the contract conditions). They are disliked by the client's quantity surveyor because the contractor is not tied to a price, although the number of hours of work claimed has to be reasonable. They are generally a prime source of argument.

He lost on another previous contract because Simon wouldn't pay for an extension of time; in fact applied the contractual right of imposing liquidated damages for a four week overrun, saying that he was worried about a current external audit being carried out on all Southwark's building works.

One of his current jobs wasn't looking too bright either. His bricklayer had pulled off the job saying that his estimator had made a balls up of the tender and he couldn't make it pay, so he had to quickly find another, which wasn't cheap. He'd had a problem with the ground works, coming across large quantities of concrete which had to be broken out, the bill of quantities had stated that the excavation should include for all necessary breaking out of such substances, which is unusual.

He had only just started another job on site, which was late in starting because his usual scaffolding company, the one he had based his tender on, had pulled out at the last minute due to a lack of labour and scaffolding tube; apparently they had been inundated with work. So he had to engage a more costly alternative.

So, George wasn't a happy bunny. He decided that enough was enough with Southwark and particularly with Simon. He was going to stitch him up. Several ideas came to mind as he mulled over differing alternatives. It didn't take him too long to work something out. Simon was vulnerable in more ways than one. In fact it was surprising he still maintained his position. The plot was quite simple, but hopefully effective.

George rang Simon at his office.
'Hello Simon, George here, I'm organising a little party at the Harvesters Hotel next Friday. There'll be a slap up meal, plenty of drink and entertainment; I understand a good local band is playing. Can I look forward to your company?'
'You bet, as it happens I'm not doing anything and the mother in-law is coming round. It'll be a great excuse to get out of the house'.

'Great, and by the way, you don't have to worry about driving home, there'll be a room reserved for you'.
'Thanks a lot George; I'll be able to sleep it off in peace'.
'See you there about eight then'
'Cheers George, I'm looking forward to it'. Replied Simon as he rang off.

The problem that George faced was that he would be implicated if he made it publicly known that Simon was bent. Furthermore, he didn't have a lot of faith in the judicial system. A few months ago a case came to court at another neighbouring London Borough of a similar nature where a contractor and a quantity surveyor were taken to court and the ridiculous outcome was that the very naive judge found it to be a coincidence that the two men involved just happened to be on the same flight and booked into the same hotel for the same period of time in Barbados. Many people couldn't believe the outcome of this case, it makes you wonder if judges are on the same planet as us, they seem to be detached from the normal street wise day to day happenings in our society.

George had a different idea and he was confident that it would work. Naturally, in doing so he ran the risk of not getting any more work from Southwark. This didn't bother him too much because he hadn't made any money lately from his most recent jobs with them.

George and Simon sat at the head of the table where dinner was served. George's quantity surveyor, Dave Potts, who was Simon's counterpart, sat beside Simon. There were four other subcontractors with them and a single female office assistant called June, who wore a short skirt, high heels and had delightful shapely legs. Simon immediately took a shine to her and she played along making eyes at him.

A band later played and Simon grabbed the opportunity to dance with June. There was plenty of drink flowing and everybody was having a whale of a time. One of George's mates was secretly taking photos of Simon enjoying himself, particularly when the slow dances came on and he was dancing close to June. He actually got a couple of shots of him with his hand up her skirt as they passionately kissed.
.
'Enjoying yourself Simon?' Dave asked when they returned to the table.

'You bet, I didn't know you had a cracker like her in your office'. He whispered back.
Dave gave a little wink as he said under his breath so only Simon could hear. 'She's game'.
Simon's eyes immediately lit up as he let out a dirty laugh.

The evening ended with Simon being led hand in hand by June up to his room. Naturally the camera was in full action. George and the boys caught taxis home having thoroughly enjoyed themselves. The plan had worked to a Tee.

Unbeknown to Simon, June had a tape rolling in her handbag recording the sounds of their sweet talk and lovemaking, which went on until the early hours of the morning. By the time Simon woke the next morning, much to his disappointment, June had gone. As far as she was concerned she had carried out her part of the deal with George successfully and knew he would be pleased with the result.

Indeed, he was delighted having listened to the recording. The photos turned out a treat as well, so all the groundwork had been completed to more than his satisfaction. Part of the final stage was put in motion. He contacted Southwark Council's Director of

Building and arranged a meeting to discuss future tenders. At the meeting George spilled the beans on Simon and was naturally hoping that the information he had would be seriously detrimental to his position. But he was wrong. The Director blew a fuse and tore into him, cursing and swearing. He was not aware of their cosy relationship and couldn't understand why he had flared up. The meeting ended with George leaving the office red faced having not damaged Simon's credibility at all.

Dave's wife Susan was a keen gardener and regularly attended the village gardeners club on a Thursday evening where she had established a circle of friends. One of these ladies was a friendly neighbour of Simon's wife. They got on very well together and she was well aware of what a pig he was to her. Apparently she had threatened to leave him if he continued to play around.

One evening after lunch, Dave asked Susan.
'Who's that lady at your gardeners club, you know, the neighbour of that fart Simon?'
'Oh, you mean Linda, why do you ask?'
Then Dave revealed all the details of the events, which was the second part of George's plan. She laughed like a drain.

'Dave, you're a real shocker, but I'm up for it, I'll phone Linda in the morning and arrange to meet for afternoon tea'
'Thanks darling, you're a gem.'

When Susan told Linda about the event at the Harvesters she was only too keen to assist in being a sympathetic neighbour and reveal all to Simon's wife, Clare, complete with the relevant photos and tape recording.

Linda knew what a devious character Simon was; on several occasions he'd had confrontations with her husband over trivial matters. She thought he was a real swine of the first order. So she popped round to see Clare with all the evidence. Clare wasn't particularly surprised or upset, but it was the first time she'd actually got concrete evidence of her husband's unfaithful activities.

So it was a visit to the solicitors who said the information would be sufficient for a divorce. It only took her a couple of days to think it over and decided that enough was enough and consequently took the necessary proceedings.

Simon was furious; he'd been set up and caught hook line and sinker. Admittedly, he no longer loved his wife, his marriage had become more of a convenience than anything else, but he knew he would miss her. No more cooked dinners and he would have to do his own washing and ironing. His whole world had crashed and he was absolutely devastated. He moved out into a bed sit, a far cry from his previous comforts.

George was pleased; thankfully he had two strings to his bow. He'd got the swine, but something or other had been on the cards for a long time; he'd been walking a fine line.

CHAPTER 6

Facet Windows & Doors were a reasonably successful organisation, based in Maidstone, Kent. They had carried out several jobs for Southwark Council and had gained themselves a good reputation. Rumour had it that the managing director, Kenny Clarke, who was in his sixties, had links with the London underworld in the '70's. This was a worrying factor when negotiating because it's in the back of your mind. Apparently, as a point of interest, they had a contract with a prison, having the inmates making up the frames for the windows.

They had been recommended to G. Turner Builders by Simon Ratcliff, which was a worry in itself. However, Dave Potts invited them to tender for a job and they won it. In fact, as it turned out they did a good job. The team of window fitters were efficient and communicated well with the tenants. The job went like a dream, their organisational skills were excellent and they completed the work ten days ahead of programme. Above all, the client was more than happy.

They started to carry out another job with Dave as the contractor's quantity surveyor, but from day one things didn't look good. In fact they started on site three weeks late with a different crew than the previous contract and they were in a right mess. They failed to follow the procedures of keeping the tenants informed and when they removed the existing wooden windows they didn't dispose of them in the skips, just left the timber on the scaffolding with broken glass as well.

This was a Health and Safety hazard which was picked up by Southwark's Clerk of the Works. He approached Dave Potts because their site agent wasn't on site. They were having problems with this particular agent at the time. So Dave attended site with the Clerk and they agreed that work should stop. It was against Health and Safety regulations not to have the site adequately supervised. Plus the mess everywhere made it a hazard.

Dave contacted Kenny about the situation and he had to admit they were having labour shortage problems. With a lot of persuasion they finally sent in a reasonably good team to hit the job, but there was a three week overrun on the job. The problems and stress caused were not forgotten, so when it came to another contract, Juniper House, they were very reluctantly invited to tender. As it turned out they were the lowest, but Dave blew them out, G. Turner Builders couldn't afford to have its reputation tarnished by a similar incident.

Kenny wasn't pleased, he had pleaded with Dave to let them have the contract, even offering a 3% discounted price, saying they had got rid of the bad crew and now had a good labour strength. But Dave wouldn't budge, as far as he was concerned it was a case of 'once bitten, twice shy'. Furthermore, he wasn't going to let Kenny's reputation bother him.

At a later date they couldn't agree the final account. So Dave was invited to Maidstone to their office to try and sort it out. He was led into their conference room where there was a large round table. He was initially on his own, but soon received a cup of tea from their secretary, closely followed by Kenny introducing himself. He only stood about five foot five, of average build and had a full head of grey wavy hair.
'So, you blew me out on the new contract!'
'I'm afraid so Kenny, We can't afford to have a similar situation arising.' Dave replied.
Kenny sat down and opened a file.
'Why won't you pay us for an extension of time, we had some extra works to do and

incurred more overheads?' Kenny said abruptly.

'The extra works only took the place of some of the work that was omitted, in actual fact we want to impose liquidated damages for the three week overrun, all in accordance with the terms and conditions of our contract.'

'So, Southwark are charging you damages then?' Kenny snapped.

'That's none of your business.'

Dave thought Kenny was going to blow a gasket, his face turned bright red with anger.'

'Listen sonny Jim, I've met your sort before and tougher, how dare you talk to me like that.'

'This is business Kenny, not a boxing match.'

Kenny forced a smile in admiration; he did not expect this opposition.

'We had a lot of problems with this contract Kenny and we didn't gain any brownie points when Southwark's Clerk of the Works forced us to stop work on site. It was a dreadful situation, a far cry and contrast to your previous job with us.'

'But we sorted it out in the end.' Kenny pleaded.

'Unfortunately the damage had already been done.'

They continued to discuss this issue further, but couldn't come to an agreement. Other outstanding items were thrashed out, most of them being agreed. So the overall final account figure was not finalised. At the end of the meeting Kenny invited Dave to have a look at their production area. Dave was surprised at what he saw. There were not many people working and it appeared they assembled all the windows by hand, which seemed a painstaking and primitive exercise.

Dave left Maidstone with not an entirely satisfactory result, but pleased he stood his ground. He wouldn't let an ex London hard man intimidate him. Anyway as far as Kenny was personally concerned, those days were over, but what contacts did he have? This was a worrying thought that started to turn in Dave's mind because Kenny definitely wasn't a happy bunny.

CHAPTER 7

One of Dave Potts's jobs was to price up tenders for jobs that came into the office. He would do this by splitting the bill of quantities into various work packages and send them out to his respective subcontractors for pricing. When he received these back he would then put together his tender based on their prices.

An interesting job came into the office for the refurbishment of three blocks of flats in Peckham. This was being financed by the Government under a new 'Capital Initiative Scheme', which was appropriately called 'Reasonable Homes to Live In'.

The work on this contract basically consisted of the replacement of windows and doors, concrete repairs, external painting, the replacement of lift systems and the resurfacing of the macadam flat roofs.

There had been two or three other similar jobs which had been already let to other contractors and one of them had received a lot of bad publicity. The reason for this was there had been no allowance for a temporary roof to be erected while the works were being carried out and it had rained a lot which seeped through to the top flats naturally causing a lot of problems. The tenants were up in arms and there had been many insurance claims against the main contractor who then had the problem of applying to the Council for reimbursement, not to mention the inconvenience of all the making good. The tender had been put together by a young inexperienced supervising officer who failed to recognise the importance of having a temporary roof for protection.

Dave was pleased he had not been successful with those tenders and was glad the specification had been revised to allow for a temporary roof. Dave was a shrewd quantity surveyor and was always looking for ways to save money to make his tender more competitive. Consequently, he arranged a meeting with Paul Anderson of Blue Arrow Scaffolding.

There was also another job that had come in for pricing for just the resurfacing of the flat roof of an eight storey block of flats which required a temporary roof which he wanted to discuss with Paul.

Paul arrived in the car park in a huge new BMW; he was obviously doing very well. He needed a big car because of his size. He stood at six foot two and had a very large build to go with it, although his belly showed signs of years of drinking. He had a mass of black curly hair showing signs of greying and he obviously hadn't shaven for a couple of days. He was a South London boy born and bred and was as hard as nails; you wouldn't want to cross his path. Although being tough he was quite laid back when negotiating tenders and prices and had done G. Turner Builders a few favours in the past.

'Hello Dave mate, are you O.K?'
'Yes fine thanks and you?'
'I'm good, now what do you want to discuss?'
'Well there are a couple of things. We've had a big tender in which requires temporary roofing while some flat roofs are resurfaced. We would like you to price the job, but I was wondering how we could save some money by not doing a complete temporary roof because obviously its not required all the time, only when they are working on a particular section?'
'Well the traditional method is to erect scaffold supports and lay corrugated sheeting over the top. But there is a system invented in Japan called Haki. You erect the supports the same but instead of having the corrugated sheeting you have large sheets of timber framed polystyrene sheeting temporarily fixed to the

supports and as you work along the roof you move the sheeting along for cover. It's successfully used a lot in Asia, particularly India. The only problem that I can foresee is if you have high winds, I'm not sure how they would stand up to that.'
'Surely if they were securely fixed, that wouldn't be a problem?'
'It can get very windy on the top of those blocks though Dave.'
'Well I think that's a risk we can take.'
Dave handed Paul his tender documents.
'Can you give me a price based on that system then please and send me some technical literature for the health and safety file.'
'No problem.' Paul replied.
'Now, I've also got an eight storey block of flats that are to have its flat roof re-felted; there's no other works at all. It seems an extremely costly exercise to scaffold all round. Can you come up with an alternative?'
'Yes, we could design a cantilever system with a handrail around the perimeter.'

Paul drew a sketch of what he meant. The rail around the outside had intermediate scaffold poles attached. These were about three metres long perpendicular to the rail weighted down with sandbags at the end.

'I think that's brilliant.' Dave commented.
'You've come up with two great ideas, now we stand a good chance of winning both jobs hopefully with reasonably high profit margins.'
'You haven't got my tender figures yet.' Paul laughed.
'O.K. then Paul, if you could visit the site to assess the scope of your work then give me a price I would be very grateful.'
'No problem, you'll hear from me soon.' Paul replied as he raised his huge body from the chair and left the office.

Paul soon returned his prices and Dave submitted his tenders on both jobs and the following week he was delighted to have won both. He had been a bit crafty because he guessed he was ahead of the market with the ideas Paul had come up with so he included in his price a sizable sum for their benefit without overdoing it and loosing the job. Things were looking good for G. Turner Builders and George thanked Dave with a bottle of his favourite rum.

CHAPTER 8

There had notoriously been problems in the past of thieves gaining access to new build sites in the early stages of the contract and stealing the ground worker's plant. The usual target was their diesel or petrol driven generators which were commonly used to supply the necessary electrical power for their tools. It should be remembered that the majority of sites in the primary stages of a contract have no power supply. For this reason, one method of protection was for the ground worker to bury his generator underground overnight by digging a pit, carefully lowering the generator using a JCB digger, covering the top with a couple of sheets of hardboard, then shovelling loose topsoil on the top.

This may appear to be a painstaking exercise, but is commonly carried out at the end of each day. In the unlikely event the potential thieves found the pit, they would have great difficulty in hoisting out the generator manually, the JCB's being either off site or securely locked. Steel containers may well be on site, but these are a common target for experienced thieves who know how to gain access. Insurance against theft is expensive; furthermore the prospect of future increases in premiums and the excess value may not make it a viable proposition to put in a claim, particularly for small less expensive items.

Tommy Stevens was an Irish ground worker, a lovely man of small build who stood about five foot six. He did a lot of work for G. Turner Builders and was currently working on a Southwark job. It was about 7.30am one morning when he was retrieving his hidden generator to start the days work when Dave Potts arrived on site.

'You're up early.' Tommy said with a smile.
'Yes, well you know what they say; the early bird catches the worm. Anyway, how are you Tommy?'
'Fine thanks Dave, and your good self.'
'Couldn't be better; now what's the problem with the ground that you've encountered?'
'Well, while digging the foundations we've hit rock about a foot down. There's loads of it and the supervising officer wants it broken out.'
'Surely the rock in itself would be a solid enough base to pour the concrete onto, don't you think?'
'Evidently not, this guy has had a similar previous experience on another job where it was found the concrete didn't spread the load sufficiently well and after six months cracks

started to develop due to differential settlement.'

'I see, so we've got to break it out. How much it will that cost?'

'That'll be about a £80 a cubic metre.' Tommy replied.

'Then there's the delay; we'll have to apply for an extension of time. Not a very good start; still these things happen. I'll contact Simon when I get back to the office and give him a price. By the way, how's the drainage job going?'

'It's almost finished; we've now been instructed to paint the copper waste pipes with black bituminous paint. Apparently it's quite a bad area for thieving and on another similar job they ripped out the pipes to sell for scrap.'

'That's a good idea, have the new drains been tested?'

'Yes, we had a bit of a problem with that deep drain that runs alongside the road, I was worried about that one, there's only a very small fall you see. But I know Reg the Supervising Officer quite well, we go back about twenty years and he was good about it saying that gravity will ease the flow. If anybody else had been on the job they could have been awkward about it, so I was quite relieved.'

'I should say, re-digging that one out at that stage would have been costly, seeing you'd already laid the drain'

'Yes, it would have taken a big chunk out of my profit margin.'

'By the way, I've had a letter from Simon saying that B.T. is claiming £1,200 for relaying those cables that were accidentally dug out.'

'That's a bit steep; they were only there for a day. Anyway, I don't reckon it was us, the cable T.V. organisation were excavating around that area at that time.'

'I know, they just assumed it was all to do with our work, Simon got the bill because of the Southwark signboard and he's naturally passed it on to us. But I'm not paying, I shall argue the point, but no doubt he'll still deduct it from our valuation. I won't pass it onto you though Tommy.'

'Thanks Dave, that's very good of you.'

Dave then drove back to the office. He had a meeting with John Woods, an argumentative quantity surveyor for Tony Andrews who was the painting subcontractor on a school. The job hadn't started very well; they had to change the specification for the paint system. The inexperienced Supervising Officer had written into the tender a paint system that required a complete burn off of the existing paint because it soaked into the timber. The tender only allowed for a part burn off of the worst loose and flaking paint.

So the benefit of this paint would not be met because the majority of the paint would be applied to only a rubbed down previously painted surface. Added to which, there was no competition when pricing for the supply of the paint because there was only one supplier specified. This naturally increased the tender price unnecessarily. The specification was changed with an architect's instruction to rub down or if necessary burn off loose and flaking paint, apply one coat primer to bare surfaces, then two undercoats and one top coat.

Simon asked Dave for a saving on the revised specification, but when he approached John he didn't want to know, which didn't surprise Dave at all knowing the character he was dealing with.

John pulled up in the car park in his blue Mercedes. He didn't look very happy as he walked in. His hair was long and straggly, it desperately needed cutting and he was unshaven and looked as though he'd been up all night, his eyes were red and had bags under them.

'Hello Dave'. He snapped.
'Hello John, you look as though you've had a rare old night.'
'Don't mention it; I was out with a load of painters on a stag night. I can't seem to handle it these days; I suppose age is catching up with me.'
'I'll make you a coffee'
As soon as Dave returned from the kitchen, John started.
'Why won't you pay for my dayworks for time lost when we can't burn off because of the children being in the classrooms?'
'You know the score John, under health and safety requirements you can only burn off when the classrooms are empty, that's written into the contract. Consequently, you should have allowed for that in your price.'
'But it takes a lot of organising with the teachers to get empty rooms available and time has been lost, I've had painters standing around doing nothing.'
'You just have to organise your labour resources accordingly, it's a big school and they could be working elsewhere, or even on another contract.'
'Yes but its all time consuming and costly.'
'You don't change John, you're so argumentative, you wont take no for an answer. Put yourself in my position, I'm not prepared

to put these dayworks for lost time forward because I know what Simon will say and I would agree with him and furthermore I don't want to make a fool of myself. You'll have to give way on this one. Anyway, you've already gained by not offering a saving on the revised paint specification. Just be grateful for that and let this one rest.'

At that point their meeting came to a close and John stomped out of the office muttering quietly to himself. He was not pleased and Dave knew it. But there were always contentious issues with this painting organisation. Occasionally they put forward a good argument and Dave paid up, but they were hard work. On the plus side they were very good painters, there were very rarely any complaints about their work. Furthermore, the men on site were courteous and had a good relationship with the site agent and they always met the programme requirements.

Dave then rang Simon.
'Hello Simon, Dave here, how are you doing?'
'Fine thanks Dave, how are things going with you?'
'Not bad, but we've hit rock on the new build job.'

'Oh no, that's all I needed to hear, is there much of it?'

'Enough to delay the programme and it'll cost you £100 a cubic metre to break it out.'

'That's what it's going to cost you, you mean.'

'No Simon, it's under ground and we weren't aware of it at tender stage. Anyway, it's a measurable item under the standard method of measurement and it's not included in the bill of quantities. Perhaps you should have put in a provisional sum for unforeseen works'

'Don't tell me how to do my job.' He snapped back. 'I'll have to contact the neighbourhood to see if there's any extra money available, but I very much doubt it, they're running on a very tight financial programme. In the meantime, you'll have to stop work until a decision is made.'

'O.k. Simon, we'll pull off the job until further notice, it'll be cheaper to do that than have men standing around doing nothing.'

So Dave rang Tommy with the news and they stopped work. A week later it was confirmed the job wouldn't go ahead until the neighbourhood could get additional funding in the next financial year, which was a big blow to all concerned.

CHAPTER 9

St. Martins School was another Southwark job that G. Turner Builders were currently working on. This was a very large Junior School which had an annex building for unfortunate children with health problems. This annex had a pitched tiled roof which had to be renewed. The main building had a flat tarmac roof which was amusing because it had a tall surrounding wall and a football pitch marked out on it, although it hadn't been used as such for many years. This surface had to be hacked up and renewed. To do this work at high level all the material had to be hoisted up and barrowed, which was a long and tedious task.

There was a problem that arose with the supply of water for these flat roofing works. When the plumber came off some pipe work he didn't cap off a supply and water was left leaking onto the roof for a whole weekend which flooded it. This seeped through the building causing damage to the classrooms. They had to be dried out and redecorated and an insurance claim was put forward.

The other works included the painting of all the timber windows and a chemical clean of the concrete surfaces. The latter was the first job to be carried out once the scaffolding was up. Before this work commenced a satisfactory risk analysis and method statement had to be drawn up for the health and safety file, which had to be approved by the Health and Safety Officer. The chemicals were jet sprayed onto the concrete and the surface cleaned with brushes. The operatives wore protective clothing and the work was carried out during the Easter holidays so that the children and staff weren't endangered.

While re-roofing a lovely pair of original terracotta chimney pots were removed. These should have been given to the school under the terms and conditions of the contract, but it ended up with the supervising officer having one and Simon Ratcliff the Southwark quantity surveyor, the other. Unfortunately, this sort of thing goes on a lot in the building game and it's usually advisable to turn a blind eye to these events.

There was a detail problem in a valley in the roof. This is where two pitched roofs along side each of the other meet along the bottom. The supervising officer was having difficulty so he called a meeting with two roofers and a Marley Tile representative. All told there must have been a combined seventy years experience advising him and he still couldn't make up his mind what to instruct. He was relatively new and inexperienced and didn't want to make a mistake. In the end they decided on the first thought of solution, the whole event was a big embarrassment.

The painting subcontractors, Magnum Painting & Decorating, were a well established Southwark organisation; they had carried out many jobs for G. Turner Builders to a very high standard in the past. Dave Potts knew their estimator and quantity surveyor Brian Palmer very well. He was a mature man in his early sixties, had been working for the firm for twenty five years and he carried out both of his work functions for his company to a high standard. Nothing out of the ordinary occurred on their contracts without Brian informing Dave; they had an excellent working relationship.

Now on school projects the caretaker plays an important role for various reasons, one of them being for gaining access, particularly out of normal school hours. His name was Albert Harvey, a very fit man of average build in his early thirties and enjoyed his whiskey, which revealed the tell tale signs of red bloodshot eyes. In order to get the job done on time it was necessary for work to be carried out outside normal school hours, for example they started at 7.30am and finished at 4.30pm, worked most Saturdays and then of course there were the school holidays. The caretaker had to be on site all the time and naturally wanted payment for these extra hours that were over and above what he would normally work. These extra hours were booked and paid for by the main contractor, G. Turner Builders, directly to the school all in accordance with the terms and conditions of the contract.

It was Dave Potts job as the contractor's quantity surveyor to book these hours and send a cheque to the school on a fortnightly basis. However, it came to light that Albert was being a naughty boy and asking Brian the painter for a backhander whenever they wanted to gain out of hour's access. This was on top of his extra payment from G. Turner Builders. Dave was absolutely furious when he learnt this from Brian and decided to do something about it; he considered it not only to be dishonest but very greedy.

So he arranged a meeting with the head mistress and told her and she was disgusted. Having considered her options she confronted Albert who admitted it, then suspended him from his duties for three months without pay, which on reflection was quite lenient because it could have resulted in instant dismissal. So the school temporarily employed another caretaker, fortunately he was loaned from another local school and had a good working knowledge of what to do.

CHAPTER 10

George Turner liked carrying out work for Local Authorities for two main reasons. There was a continuous flow of work which didn't appear to fluctuate too much, even in recessionary periods they still had a yearly allowance to spend. But the most important reason was they wouldn't go bankrupt and he was guaranteed his money. They were his bread and butter, albeit he could potentially make a lot more money working in the private sector, but it was risky, he knew of several similar building organisations that had gone to the wall because they had carried out a lot of work for clients who had run out of money and couldn't afford to pay them. This often occurred during a recession.

Another thing that George believed in was the old cliché 'don't put all your eggs in one basket.' So, as well as contracting for Southwark, he also carried out work for the London Borough of Lambeth, which is London's largest Borough. The work in both Boroughs was of a similar nature, apart from one contract he had with Lambeth which was a 'measured term' contract for the alteration of existing council houses, measured using the 'National Schedule of Rates.'

Measured term contracts are let for a period of time, which can be six months, one, two or three years. The work carried out is instructed on a works order and measured after completion using a schedule of rates. A lot of maintenance work is done in this manner. The measurement of these works is essentially a specialist quantity surveyors job.

The contract that G. Turner Builders had with Lambeth was for one year, with the opportunity to negotiate a further year if both parties were happy to do so. Dave Potts had worked on measured term contracts before, so he was no stranger to it. But he had his work cut out on other contracts so George took on a freelance surveyor just to do this work.

His name was Andy Stock, a smartly dressed man in his mid thirties, but he had a temperament problem, which didn't go down too well in the camp. There was also a conflict of personalities between him and Dave and to make matters worse he was envious of his full time contract of employment, stating that he thought it was unfair that he was only employed on a part time basis with no holiday entitlement or sick pay and one weeks notice either way.

Furthermore, there had been complaints about the way he conducted himself from the client, which George obviously wasn't pleased about. Also, he wasn't keeping up with his work and the monthly figures weren't looking too good.

Consequently, whilst Andy was out of the office, Dave had a look at his work and picked up on many items he had missed in his measures, (an item of work measured using the schedule is built up with several rates) and there were quite a few arithmetical errors.

So one morning Dave queried Andy about his work.
'I've had a look at some of your measures Andy and I'm not too happy with them.'
'Do you mean to say you've been through my desk while I'm not here?'
'No I haven't been through your desk, I wouldn't do that. All I did was look through one of your work files from the shelf over there.' Dave replied pointing in the direction of a bundle of files on the shelf above Andy's desk.
'I see, so you don't trust me?' Andy said angrily.
'No, it's not that I don't trust you, it's just that we're not making any money on your contract and I was trying to pinpoint a reason why.'

'Oh I see, that's a bit sneaky isn't it. You might have consulted me first and then perhaps we could have had a look together.'

'Dave was working under my instruction and his findings don't look good.' George said as he walked into the room.

'As you're fully aware, with measured term using the schedule of rates it's very important not to miss anything because they all add up and unfortunately at the end of the day that's why we're loosing money.' Dave commented.

'Bullshit, the pair of you have got it in for me. I have to put up with enough here under the terms and conditions of my employment contract and I don't need some little toe rag like you telling me how to do my job.' Andy shouted back.

'You agreed with the conditions of employment when you started with us and at the time I seem to remember you were very grateful for the work.' George replied.

'Yeah, well that was then. Now I've learnt the conditions that you employ Dave on, I think I'm treated very unfairly.' Andy replied in slightly a lower tone. He was obviously feeling very sorry for himself.

'Dave has been with us a good number of years, he's a good hard worker and has earned his entitlement and you've only been here five minutes. Besides, I don't have to substantiate my employment strategies with the likes of you, that's none of your business.' George said raising his voice and head so he was looking down on Andy. He was not at all amused and you could feel a definite air of tension in the room.

Andy snapped and banged his clenched fist on the table. 'So, what's it to be then?' He barked.
George replied very slowly, carefully choosing his words. 'I think you had better clear your desk and get the hell out of here.'
At which point Andy grabbed hold of his desk and tipped it right over so that it went crashing to the floor. George saw it coming and sidestepped out of the way.
'Bollocks to the pair of you, you haven't heard the last of this.' Andy shouted as he went steaming out of the office, slamming the door behind him. There was a few moments silence as the air appeared to cool.
'Well I'm glad we've got him out of the way.' George said to Dave.
'Yeah and he certainly knows how to get himself worked up, which isn't good in a work situation.' Dave replied.
'What do you suggest we do now with this contract?' George asked.

'Well we've almost finished the first term and I think we should bail out then without renewing the contract for another term. That way at least we keep the client happy by not defaulting. Regarding the measuring, I'll just have to fit it in myself.'
'Good reasoning.' George replied. 'Thanks very much for helping me out.'
'That's what I'm paid for.' Dave said with a smile on his face.

CHAPTER 11

The Fountain is basically a local's pub situated on the Rotherithe High Road, just round the corner from Debnams Road in Southwark. It had a pool table, a juke box and the usual couple of fruit machines. It was in desperate need of redecoration, the toilets were quite revolting and the majority of the fitted carpet was threadbare. All in all, it could hardly be regarded as a crowd puller, in fact possibly its only main attraction was the cheap beer. You certainly wouldn't score many points taking a young lady there.

Dave Potts popped in there occasionally when he was in the area and in need of a little alcoholic nourishment. He preferred it to the more upmarket busy pubs because he knew he could have a quiet pint without being disturbed giving him time to gather his thoughts.

He walked in one lunch time and was pleased to hear his favourite single being played; Space Oddity by David Bowie. Dave was humming the tune while waiting at the bar and smiled at the unshaven man sitting on a stool next to him, who nodded in response.

'They don't make them like this anymore.' Dave said.
'They sure don't, can't understand what they see in the music of today.' The man replied.
'Perhaps we're just getting old.' The barman said having now got Dave's attention.
'Pint of bitter and a packet of cheese and onion crisps please.' Dave politely requested.
Just then Brown Sugar by The Rolling Stones came on.
'Another great oldie.' Dave remarked.

The juke box was another reason why Dave liked this pub; it helped put the pressures of work out of his mind. The barman served Dave his pint and crisps.

'Would you like a game of pool?' The man sitting next to Dave asked.
'Yeah, why not.' Dave replied digging in his pocket for a pound coin.

They set the balls up and broke off. After a couple of shots Dave realised the man had played the game before, he was deliberately trying to cover the pockets with his nominated striped balls. Mind you, Dave was a dab hand at snooker; his highest break was seventy six, which is above average at club level. His potting skills were second to none, but pool is

an entirely different ball game, especially when your potting line is blocked by your opponent's balls. So it ended up a very tactical affair, with Dave potting the black to only just win.
'That was a good game.' Dave remarked.
'Yes but I think you're a better potter than me.' The man replied.
'Looks like I'm playing you then Potts boy.' Came a stern rough voice from the end of the bar.

Dave hadn't noticed because he was taking a shot at the time, but this particular person had placed a pound coin on the side of the table, which means he has challenged the winner.

'Do I know you?' Dave queried.
'You've probably forgotten, but you gave me the push a couple of years ago. I was a labourer working on Craig Court. The name's Barney Hibbs.'

Dave froze, he could feel his heart beating faster and his rear end was pouting, the last thing he wanted was a confrontation with any of the Hibbs family, they had a dreadful reputation for street fighting.

'Oh of course I remember you Barney. You were a good hard worker. I seem to remember you had a fight with one of the carpenters.'

'Yes that's right; the swine wound me up so much I lost my rag.' Barney replied.

'That carpenter was nothing but a nuisance; he caused us a lot of problems, so much so we got rid of him in the end. If we had realised what he was like at an earlier stage then perhaps the unfortunate event with you wouldn't have occurred. As it happens we need good workers like you, why don't you call into the office, I'm sure we could fix you up with something.' Dave said seriously hoping that Barney would take him up on that.

'Well thanks very much, I think I'll do that.' Barney replied walking towards the pool table with a smile on his face.

Dave felt extremely relieved that he had successfully defused a very difficult situation. He set the balls up and broke off being not too sure whether to play his proper game or let Barney win. He decided to play his usual game because Barney was no fool and he wouldn't have liked it any other way.

'Can I get you a drink Barney?' Dave asked as he potted his third successive ball.

'Yeah, I'll have a Scotch and Soda.' He replied.

The game didn't take long to finish with Barney potting the black to win. He sank his Scotch and turned towards Dave.
'Thanks for that, aren't you having one?'
'No, got to watch the drink driving.' Dave replied.
'Yeah, I suppose a surveyor without a licence isn't much good to anybody.' Barney said.
'Your right there, the old Bill are pretty hot these days. Anyway, hopefully you'll be back on the cards again shortly. I'll tell George to expect you.' Dave said sinking the remainder of his pint.
'Yeah, you do that. I won't let you down. You're not going Peckham way by any chance?' Barney enquired.
'Yes I am, why do you want a lift?'
'If it's not too much trouble, only I've had a bit of a skin full and I'd prefer to leave my car parked up.' Barney replied.

So they left the pub and made their way to Dave's car. They hadn't walked far when they came across a major disturbance in the road. A white armoured van, the type used to transport prisoners, was being held up by two armed masked men shouting at the driver to get out of the vehicle. Only a few seconds later, although it seemed like minutes, one of the gunmen fired his gun into the side of the van to let them know they meant business. The uniformed driver carefully got out of the van with his hands in the air shouting 'don't shoot, don't shoot.'

'Just keep still and don't say anything.' Barney instructed Dave.

There were a few bystanders who were amazed at what they were witnessing. They were also motionless.

'Now open the back of the van.' One of the gunmen ordered.

The driver did exactly as he was told; it would have been foolish to do anything else as these men meant business. Out jumped a handcuffed young man in his early twenties. He ran to the waiting car which had stopped the van, closely followed by the two armed men. By this time police sirens could be heard not far away. All three jumped into the car which sped off at high speed.

The police were approaching from behind trying desperately hard to get to the scene through the held up traffic, gradually weaving their way through. The driver of the van was being comforted by a few people and a kind lady brought him out a cup of tea to steady his nerves. The ordeal had been quite a shock for everybody. It seemed ages before the police arrived, but there wasn't much they could do apart from taking down the details of the getaway car. By this time Dave and Barney were well out of the way travelling to Peckham.

It was headline news that evening on the television. Apparently, the man who escaped had recently been sentenced for armed robbery, not the sort of person to tangle with. The whole incident had been carefully planned. The police had recovered the getaway car which had been stolen. They were all still at large. There was a photo of the escaped prisoner, he was described as dangerous and should not be approached by the public.

Three weeks later he was recaptured. The police had received a tip off that he was hiding out in a flat on an estate in Bermondsey. They made their raid at four in the morning, which was timed deliberately so that hopefully the occupants were in a deep sleep, which they were. So his freedom hadn't lasted long, the whole episode had really been a waste of time; thankfully nobody was hurt.

CHAPTER 12

Having interviewed Tim, Chief Inspector Blake spent the rest of the morning interviewing the other site operatives. Three of them had seen two men matching the description Tim had given hastily boarding a white transit van and driving off at speed. They were heading towards the Old Kent Road.

'We have CCTV cameras on that road.' Blake said smiling to one of his delegates. 'I want you to spend the rest of the day recording the number plates of all the white transit vans you see on the scans for the period in question.'
'Got you boss.' Replied the Inspector and sat down in front of his computer obeying his instruction.

Two hours later he was knocking on Blake's door.
'I've got seven of them, but there's one in particular who appears to be speeding and driving erratically. It's registered to a Peckham man.'
'Right, let's pay him a visit.' Blake replied grabbing hold of his jacket as they walked out.

It only took them a few minutes to get there; it was a flat in a large block. Blake hammered on the door and it was soon opened by a tall slim man with long wavy blond hair in his late twenties, definitely not answering Tim's description. Blake made their introduction.

'Good afternoon Sir, I'm Chief Inspector Blake and this is Inspector Jones. Are you the owner of a white transit van registration P648 STP?'
'Yes I am, I'm fully taxed and insured, so what's the problem.'
'Do you mind if we come in to ask you some questions?'
They entered the flat and sat in the lounge.
'Where is your van now and where were you this morning?'
'A friend of mine has borrowed it for a couple of days and I've been in all morning sleeping. I work nights you see.'

The friend appeared to answer the description Tim had given of one of the men. So they got his address, which was local and went round to his house, only to find nobody was in. So Blake put twenty four hour surveillance on the building.

By the next day they had made an arrest of a man fitting the description of one of the attackers. His name was Harry Spurgeon. Tim was invited back down the station and picked him out of an ID parade. So they had one of their men.

He was a hard stubborn man and only answered a few questions. They established that he was unemployed and had a drug habit. He had previous form for grievous bodily harm and various other assaults. He also occasionally worked under a false name as a bouncer in a night club.

What they couldn't do was establish a connection or motive for the attempted murder, nor would he reveal who his accomplice was. Blake thought he was being paid by somebody else, but there was no evidence of that on his bank statements, nor any money in the house.

Blake had good grounds for a prosecution, but his experience told him this was the tip of the iceberg, there was much more to this case than met the eye. The problem was how he would be able to progress further.

He tried the old trick of false bribery stating that the Court would be more lenient in their sentencing if he cooperated. But that didn't work. He was not only protecting his accomplice, but also his employer. Blake knew from previous similar cases that employees usually received a percentage of their payment before the job, the majority being paid after a successful execution. But fortunately it had gone pear shaped.

Perhaps in this instance all the money was being paid at the end of the job? He had no way of knowing. Things would have been considerably easier if they had his partner as well, then they could question them individually and play one against the other. Historically this provided fruitful results, but it wasn't to be.

Dave Potts was spending a few days in hospital as advised. He was suffering from shock and a very sore head. He'd had some scans which thankfully showed that he hadn't sustained any permanent damage. He was allowed a short visit from an inspector who had a photograph of the man in custody, but he said he'd never seen him before, which was no surprise.

The police wanted to bring a charge of attempted murder. The case went to Court and that was the judge's verdict sentencing him to seven years in prison, commenting that it would have been less if he had been helpful with the police enquiries.

But that's not the end of the story. The surveillance on the accused house had continued after his arrest and a young blond was spotted entering with keys. She was immediately arrested and taken down the station for questioning.

CHAPTER 13

Dave was gradually recovering from his ordeal at home being nursed by his wife Susan. He'd spent three days in hospital before he was discharged after the doctors were happy for him to do so. A nurse from his G.P. surgery called on a daily basis to redress his head wound. He had a bit of a headache, which is hardly surprising and considered himself to be very fortunate that things weren't any worse.

He had mulled over in his mind who would want to try and kill him. Fair enough, he'd had confrontations in his work capacity, probably more so recently, but to pinpoint somebody he'd upset so much that he wanted to take his life was difficult.

Paul Anderson paid him a visit one morning; Susan invited him into the lounge.
'Someone to see you Darling.' She said.
Paul walked in having to duck slightly as he did so.
'Hi Dave, how are you feeling.'
'Not too bad thanks Paul.'
'I can't understand anybody wanting to do this to you.'
'No, it's a bit of a mystery.'

'We know a lot of locals and we're keeping our ears to the ground, but haven't heard anything yet.'
'Thanks Paul.'
'I'd like to get my hands on them.' Paul said waving a clenched fist in the air.
'Yes, I certainly was lucky, if Tim hadn't turned up at that moment I wouldn't be sitting here now.'
'Very strange isn't it, they definitely had it in for you.'
They chatted for a further twenty minutes and then Paul rose to leave.
'Better be going now, you take care.'
'O.K. Paul thanks very much for popping round.'
Paul saw himself out and Dave thought that if anybody could find out who was behind this it would be him.

Chief Inspector Blake called round one afternoon and introduced himself and a police constable who accompanied him. He'd brought a bunch of flowers which Susan gratefully put in a vase and arranged them amongst many others they had received.
'Hello Mr. Potts, I'm Chief Inspector Blake and am running this case and this is P.C. Peters.'
'Just call me Dave.' He replied.

'O.K. Dave, now as you are aware we've caught one of them, the one my inspector showed you a photograph of while you were in hospital.'

'Yes, unfortunately I've never seen him before.'

'Well, he's a Peckham man, hard as nails and he won't talk. So we don't even know who his accomplice was or who's behind it all. We've been keeping our ears to the ground with our local informant network, but that hasn't shed much light. He's a small time crook, wheeling and dealing in soft drugs, a very aggressive man with form for grievous bodily harm. Not a very nice person at all. Now what I need is a list of anybody you can think of who might possibly have a motive and details of anything unusual or out of the ordinary that has occurred in your life recently.'

'There are several people that come to mind that I've had confrontations with, but only in my work capacity. For example………'

P.C. Peters was making notes in shorthand as Dave responded. After twenty minutes Susan came into the lounge with a tray of gratefully received refreshments.

'Ah, that's very kind of you Mrs. Potts.' Blake said as he reached out for the tea pot. Dave continued to talk while sipping his coffee.

'Regarding anything unusual that has occurred recently, there's my theory about a remedy for rheumatoid arthritis.'
'Oh yes of course, I remember reading about it in the papers.' Blake replied.
Dave continued to tell them about this event but iterated that there hadn't been any confrontational issues.

Blake and Peters left Dave's house having spent about an hour and a half there. They had gathered quite a lot of useful information to continue their enquiries with.

CHAPTER 14

Two weeks had now passed since the ordeal and Dave was feeling a lot better. The nurses had stopped coming round to treat him and he and Susan decided they wanted a well deserved break away from home. Kings Lynn had been a favourite place for them to visit, so they booked up for three nights at the Ramada Hotel.

Susan packed their bags which seemed substantial for their stay, but she was very much a 'we'd better take this, just in case'. Dave rang Chief Inspector Blake informing him of his intentions and they exchanged mobile numbers to maintain contact.

So off they drove with Susan at the wheel. They hadn't driven far when a feeling of relief came over them, as if they'd left all the past behind. That's the purpose of short breaks or holidays and it certainly worked. They stopped on route at a picnic spot in Thetford Forest and ate some sandwiches and drank tea from a pre-prepared flask. They went for a walk to ease their aching muscles from the drive and relieve themselves when they spotted a rare site amongst the trees and undergrowth, a wild pig.

Unfortunately, they did not have their camera with them to capture the site.

After a break of three quarters of an hour they were back on the road and it only took half an hour to reach their destination because the roads were fairly clear. They unloaded their car and checked in. They were pleased to have a room on the first floor with a pleasant view at the back of the hotel. There were loads of rabbits running around which enhanced the rural feeling of the area.

They both showered and had a change of clothes and laid back on their twin bed and watched a little T.V. Dave dozed off for half an hour and woke feeling thirsty, so they made some coffee with the provisions that had been supplied.

They then decided to socialise a bit and ventured to the bar area. There were several business people having various discussions, it appeared to be a popular place for doing so. A German couple were sitting at the bar both drinking lager from pint glasses, they were having difficulty communicating with a French couple, it appeared none of them fully understood the others language, although they could speak a little English; the conversation was amusing to say the least. The elderly male German was obviously feeling the effects of his alcohol consumption because his speech was very slurred and after a period of time was helped off his bar stool and assisted back to their room by his partner who had a fit of the giggles.

Dave offered the French couple a drink which they gladly accepted and they soon got into conversation which was greatly helped by Susan who fortunately spoke good French. Apparently they weren't actually an item but had met at a stroke unit in Paris. He had been working too hard as a coach driver and she was an overworked rheumatology consultant. Her work naturally intrigued Dave and she was amazed to have actually have met the man with the new theory. Apparently in France there had been a pharmaceutical development organisation originally working on similar lines.

Susan spoke about the lovely week she and Dave had had in Paris.
'They were so helpful.' She said.
'At the railway station when we arrived on Eurostar, there was an attendant who noticed Dave's mobility problem and offered to help. He said he was employed specifically for that

purpose and he helped us with the luggage and got us a taxi by skipping the queues of people waiting. The drive to our hotel was an experience in itself; he drove so fast dodging in and out of the cars.'

'In Paris they drive very fast.' The Frenchman responded in broken English.

'It's quite expensive as well, although they do have some lovely clothes, I bought two beautiful pairs of shoes there in a sale, actually they were very reasonably priced.' Dave remarked.

'We had a day out to the Louvre Museum, but when we got there it was shut because it was a Tuesday, the only day of the week they were closed.' Susan said and they all laughed.

They continued their conversation for about an hour then the French pair retired to their rooms. Dave and Susan decided to have their evening meal at the hotel, they were feeling fairly tired and didn't want the hassle of finding an alternative place to eat. They then also retired to their room, watched a little T.V. then went to bed.

The next morning they were both up at the crack of dawn, had a wash and got dressed then sauntered into the breakfast lounge. They were surprised to see the pair of Germans so early, but they looked a little worse for wear. Having eaten a full English breakfast they ventured out into Kings Lynn. Because of Dave's arthritis he has a mobility problem, so they were pleased to be able to hire an electric scooter from the Shopmobility facility, otherwise Dave would have found things very difficult walking for long periods around the town.

The town centre had gone through a redevelopment phase since their last visit with lots of new shops to browse through. The people were far more friendly and approachable than London, which is why they liked it there. Their favourite haunts were the charity shops where they could pick up a bargain or two. Also, it gave Dave an opportunity to sort through and hopefully add to his vinyl record collection.

It was when they stopped for a break and were drinking tea that Dave commented that he had an irritating feeling.
'I think we're being followed.' He said.
'Aren't you being a little bit sensitive?' Susan enquired.
'No, I don't think so. Don't look round.' Dave ordered as he discretely took his camera out of its case and took a couple of snaps over Susan's shoulder, then hid it out of the way.

'Finish your tea.' Dave said sharply.
'Why, where are we going?' Susan asked.
'I'm going to get these photos developed.' Dave replied.

After getting the photos developed they decided to call it a day and returned the scooter to its base and much to their surprise there was only a pound charge with the opportunity for a donation, which was marvellous value for money, so Dave slipped a fiver in the box.

Having driven back to the hotel they bumped into the French couple.
'Did you see your friend?' They enquired.
This took Dave and Susan by surprise because very few people knew they were there and they certainly hadn't arranged to meet anybody.
'There was a man asking about you earlier today.' They continued to say.
Dave fumbled in his inside pocket for the photos he had just had developed and showed them the picture of the man he had taken.
'Was this him?' He asked.
'Yes that's him, so you did see him then.' The French lady replied.
'Sort of.' Dave commented.
'Now if you could excuse us but we've had a busy day.' Dave said and then he and Susan went back to their room.

'That's incredible, so you were right in your observations.' Susan said.
'Yes, I must ring Chief Inspector Blake.' Dave said picking his mobile out of his pocket.

Chief Inspector Blake was deeply concerned when Dave rang and instructed him to return home immediately. So they checked out of the hotel and drove straight back. It was now late evening so they bought some fish and chips and relaxed from their drive. They both felt a lot more comfortable now they were on home territory.

Dave scanned the photos of the man and emailed them to Blake so he would be able to see them first thing the next morning. They then watched a little T.V. but were unable to concentrate, mainly due to tiredness and consequently decided the best thing was to get a good night's sleep, so they retired to their comfy bed.

CHAPTER 15

As soon as they returned to the station from visiting Dave Potts at his home, Blake delegated the task to a small team of three of finding out as much information as possible about Dave Potts's theory for the remedy for rheumatoid arthritis. They acted quickly and arranged an interview with the manager of the Arthritis Research Council, together with gathering all the press cuttings.

Meanwhile Blake called in Simon Ratcliff to question.
'So, you're now living on your own having been divorced.' Blake said to Simon.
'Yes, that's right, I got set up with another woman and they told my wife.' Simon replied.
'Who are they?' Blake asked.
'Bloody George Turner of G. Turner Builders, Dave Potts was also involved. They also unsuccessfully tried to get me the sack from my job.'
'Really and why would they want to do that?'
Simon looked embarrassed as he carefully replied.
'Well, they weren't happy about the payments on some of their jobs. This occurs quite frequently in the building game.'

'Is that all?' Blake pried giving the impression he knew there was more to the story.

Simon was beginning to look more uncomfortable as he replied.

'All right, I've been a naughty boy asking for backhanders, but that was from George Turner, which isn't really relevant to your enquiries.'

'But for some unknown reason this didn't affect your position of employment, did it Mr. Ratcliff.'

Simon went bright red as he responded.

'That's because the Chief Housing Officer and I are more than just good friends.'

'Oh I see, so you swing both ways.'

'I don't see what relevance my private life has to do with this case.' Simon replied angrily.

'No you probably wouldn't. Tell me Mr. Ratcliff, what are your personal feelings towards Mr. Potts.'

'My relationship with Dave Potts is purely professional and I don't have any feelings for him in the manner that you are suggesting, in fact despite his participation in ruining my marriage I certainly wouldn't wish any harm to come of him. I think your barking up the wrong tree, as you can obviously see from your records I don't have any previous convictions of that nature, in fact all I can boast of is a motoring speeding offence eight years ago.' Simon snapped back.

'O.K. Mr. Ratcliff, that will be all for now, but I will require a copy of all your bank statements for the past six months.'
'What on earth for?' Simon queried.
'That's a police matter, but I may as well tell you that we are looking for the movement of sizeable sums of money.'
Simon grumpily left the station and returned to his accommodation.

Kenny Clarke didn't show much sympathy for Dave, but then again he was made of tough meat. Having said that, being brought in for questioning had rattled his cage.
'Don't know why I'm here, you've got nothing on me.' He angrily blurted out.
'You're a suspect for his attempted murder.' Blake replied.
'Come off it, I've got too much to lose.'
'Oh yes, like your impeccable record.' Blake responded with raised eyebrows.
'God, that was years ago; I'm a respectable businessman now.' Kenny boasted.
'There's never been anything respectable about you Mr. Clarke. You've done form for grievous bodily harm, handling stolen goods and running a protection racket.'
'That was in the 60's and 70's. I've been clean for over thirty years; that's a young man's game.'

'In my book a leopard doesn't change its spots. Now tell us a bit about the confrontation you had with Dave Potts.' Blake replied, trying to break him a bit to ease the tension. But Kenny wasn't having any of it.

'Look, I had nothing to do with this and you've got nothing on me. O.K., we had disagreements on certain items of work and as a consequence of us not performing very well on a contract he blew us out on a new one. It happens from time to time, competition is fierce in the building world, but I wouldn't harm him, what he did wouldn't warrant that, after all he's basically a nice guy doing his job. I used to tangle with blokes who were asking for a good hiding and that's what they got if they messed with me. Not respectable professional people like Dave. What's more, I came here peacefully to hopefully assist you with your enquiries and all you're doing is treating me like shit by dragging up a load of old dirt. Now I want to contact my solicitor.'

'That won't be necessary Mr. Clarke, you can go now, but we will need a copy of your personal and business bank accounts.'

'No bloody problem.' Kenny said in a raised voice as he rose from his chair and marched out of the station.

Blake had interviewed two people who were possible suspects, but years of experienced and a sixth sense told him that it was unlikely that either of them were involved. But it was early days yet.

CHAPTER 16

John Woods sat slouched in a chair in the interview room, looking the worst for wear; probably nursing a hangover.
'Well Mr. Woods, we understand you got a bit steamed up on your previous meeting with Mr. Potts.' Blake said having made the formal introductions.
'That's right, he really got my back up, wouldn't be reasonable at all. All I want is fair pay for our men's work and do you think I could get it? No, I bloody couldn't, the tight sod wouldn't budge an inch. So we had a bit of a barney.'
'So as an afterthought you took matters further.' Blake prompted.
'Don't be silly, I wouldn't do that.' John shouted back.
'So what would you have done?' Blake queried.
'I wouldn't do anything like that.' He snapped back.
'You don't seem the sort of chap that would just let an incidence like that just ride Mr. Woods.' Blake replied, gradually getting a feeling of the sort of person John was.
'Don't get me wrong, I wouldn't forget the contentious issues. I'd probably keep them up my sleeve for another day, one when he needs

me to help him out, and then I'd fire away.' John replied in a more relaxed tone.

'I see, a diplomatic move held in reserve until the right time arises.' Blake replied.

'That's right, nothing physical.' John said in a much quieter voice and tone.

'We note that you have on record two individual incidences of disorderly conduct and actual bodily harm.' Blake queried prompting John to elaborate.

'Yes I had a bit too much to drink at a party one New Years Eve and this bloke was winding me up by dancing with my bird, so I just pushed him and he stumbled and fell over. He didn't hurt himself much, but he brought a charge against me for actual bodily harm. The disorderly conduct charge was brought against me by the police when I blew my top when somebody driving carelessly drove into the back of me; he was travelling far too close. As you are probably already aware, both were relatively minor incidences.'

'Yes, we've got the details and for the moment I've come to the conclusion that you had nothing to do with the incidence we are investigating Mr. Woods. Thanks very much for being cooperative. You can go now.'

John didn't say anything further; he just nodded as he rose from his chair and left the station.

Andy Stock walked swiftly into the interview room, closely followed by Blake, and sat down with a thump.

'Now then Mr. Stock, I'm Chief Inspector Blake and you've been brought here to assist us in our inquiries of the attempted murder of Mr. David Potts. Were you aware of this incidence?'

'Yeah, sure I am, it's been well publicised.'

'We understand that you were a work colleague of Mr. Potts for a relatively short period of time.' Blake prompted.

'That's right, but things didn't work out.' Andy responded.

'Really, why was that?' Blake gently queried.

'Well, I wasn't happy with my terms and conditions of employment, added to the fact that Dave Potts always seemed to be looking over my shoulder, which I wasn't comfortable about.'

'Please continue.' Blake said knowing there was more to the story.

'It all came to a crunch one day when the boss, George Turner, intervened when Dave and I were having a heated argument about an issue and he sacked me.' Andy coolly replied.

'Apparently, you really lost your rag Mr. Stock.' Blake said trying to get Andy too elaborate further.

'O.k. so I lost my temper, which isn't surprising considering I'd just been fired.' Andy snapped back.

'You turned your desk over before storming out saying they hadn't heard the last of it. What were your intentions Mr. Stock?' Blake added having seen that Andy's feathers were now ruffled.

'Well, my intention at the time was to take some form of legal action against them for unfair dismissal.'

'But you don't appear to have any grounds for that do you Mr. Stock? No, I think your intentions were of a far more aggressive nature, probably physical.' Blake prompted.

'You don't have any evidence of that though do you Chief Inspector Blake?'

'Maybe not at the moment, but rest assured Mr. Stock it's early days yet in our investigation and we've already successfully imprisoned one person. So we're hot on the trail and I'm confident we'll get to the bottom of this case very soon. Furthermore, currently your response to our questioning puts you high on our list of likely suspects for instigating this attempted murder.' Blake angrily responded, annoyed at Andy's arrogance.

'Before we go any further I'd like a solicitor to be present.' Andy responded.

'We're going to bring this interview to an end now, to give us an opportunity to carry out further ground work on you Mr. Stock.' Blake replied, which was a bit of a lie to let Andy know he hadn't heard the last of this case.
'Also, we require a copy of your bank statements.' Blake demanded.
So Andy Stock was led out of the station and Blake decided to have him under surveillance which he hoped might prove to be fruitful.

When Barney Hibbs was interviewed he was very surprised at the whole ordeal.
'He's such a nice guy. I can't imagine anybody wanting to hurt him. You know he even gave me my job back and I must admit I didn't really deserve it, lovely guy.' He stated.
'So you've never really had a confrontation with him?' Blake enquired.
'Only when he gave me the sack, but that wasn't his fault. I bumped into him down the Fountain, got talking to him and he reinstated me saying there had been a misunderstanding. I just can't fault the guy. I'd like to get my hands on whoever's behind all this.' Barney replied.
'Yes well your not alone in your thoughts, others have said similar things. So you can't think of anybody with a strong enough grudge to organise what has occurred?' Blake asked.

'No I can't.' He replied.
'O.K. Mr. Hibbs, that will be all and thank you very much for your time.'
'It's a pleasure.' Barney replied as he got up to leave.

CHAPTER 17

The next person to be led into the interview room was the school caretaker, Albert Harvey.
'Good afternoon Mr. Harvey. As you are probably aware we are currently questioning people in connection with the attempted murder of Dave Potts. You have been brought in because of the contact you had with Mr. Potts on a contract that his firm G. Turner Builders had at St. Martins School, where at the time you were employed as a caretaker.'
Albert uncomfortably crossed his legs and reached over for a cup of water before responding.
'I'm still employed, but been suspended.'
'I see and how did your suspension occur.'
'I got my wrists slapped for being a naughty boy.'
'Will you please elaborate Mr. Harvey?'
'I was receiving small backhanders from the painting subcontractor and I got found out. In actual fact it was Dave Potts who grassed me up, but I wouldn't do anything to harm him.'
'I don't know if you read the papers, but we've successfully convicted one man, but there were two of them and you don't meet the others' description. In actual fact, despite any hard feelings you may have towards Mr. Potts, at

this stage of our investigation we don't think you were involved at all.'

'Then why am I here.' Albert interrupted.

'Well we know you're a well established local man and I want you to carefully look at this photograph and tell me if you recognise him.'

Albert immediately responded.

'Yeah, I've seen him around a lot; he's a local hard man, hangs around with another geezer.'

Blake couldn't have hoped for a better reaction.

'If you could help us catch him by coming out with us and identifying him, I'll do all I can to get your employment reinstated?'

'It's a deal, I don't like the pair of them anyway, and they make me feel uncomfortable.' Albert replied.

Blake and Albert were accompanied by two plain clothed heavy policemen as they drove through Peckham in an unmarked police car.

'They usually hang out at the Old Nags Head, we'll try there first.' Albert suggested.

They pulled up on double yellow lines in a busy street near the pub and Albert jumped out. You can bet your bottom dollar that a traffic warden would appear just at the wrong time and sure enough one did. Blake swiftly displayed his badge and gave her a wink. She got the message and continued to walk on, not even glancing back.

Only a minute or two had passed and Albert was back.

'I've eyeballed him; he's playing the fruit machine by the door as you walk in.'

'O.K. Albert, now make yourself scarce and thanks very much.' Blake responded.

Albert quickly left the car closely followed by the two heavies; Blake remained in the driver's seat. There was a big scuffle as they dragged him handcuffed out of the pub and into the car. He was cursing and swearing and as Blake drove off he smiled in amusement as he saw the traffic warden peeping round the next corner.

Tim Brooks gave a positive identification, so they had now successfully caught both men involved in the incident. When questioned, he was not forthcoming as to the reason he had attacked Dave Potts, in fact like his accomplice he said very little. This frustrated Blake, but at least they were making progress.

As promised, Blake phoned the head mistress of St. Martins School and explained what a great help Albert Harvey had been to them and she agreed to reinstate his employment conditions from immediate effect and turn a blind eye to his previous wrong doing. This pleased her immensely because as she stated to

Blake he was a good caretaker and would be very difficult to replace.

CHAPTER 18

Chief Inspector Blake opened his email inbox to find one from Dave Potts with an attached photo of the person who had been following him, as he had expected. He then delegated to a couple of officers to do a D.V.L.A. search of the photo. Hopefully they might come up with something.

A seminar was held at the police station with all the team involved in the case. The three officers who had visited the manager of the Arthritis Research Council were asked to report on their findings. One of them stood up and read from a set of notes they had prepared.

'It appears that an organisation called Glyced Pharmaceuticals had spent millions of pounds developing a drug for rheumatoid arthritis sufferers. This drug kills off the antibody in the blood which attacks good tissues in the joints. In doing so it reduces the recipient's immune system causing potentially other health problems. Consequently, it was a major source of debate; it had its supporters, but also many critics, many of whom were wary that the drug could potentially cause a lot of problems in the patient's future health, which is understandable.' The officer paused for a few moments and drank from a glass of water before continuing.

'However, they heavily promoted this drug and launched it in the spring of 2007 having been given the seal of approval by the British Medical Association. Glyced's research laboratories had worked for eight years developing this drug and it was widely accepted as a major breakthrough in the treatment of R.A. An actuary had been employed who forecast that it would take five years to cover their development costs.' He paused once again.

'Apparently, Glyced is a reasonably wealthy company but they didn't want to put all their eggs in one basket; so they invested 50% of their own capital and borrowed the remainder from a private investor. The private investor was a man by the name of Jimmy Warren, a ruthless successful business man who had made a small fortune in other similar lucrative deals. Word has it that this was his planned retirement investment; he had taken a big gamble with this transaction staking 85% of his capital. So he desperately wanted it to work and things were looking good so far. Then out of the blue Dave Potts's theory came along to rock the boat.' Having completed his presentation the officer sat down.

'Thanks very much, that's interesting.' Blake commented. 'Does Warren have any form?'
'No Sir, clean as a whistle.' Another officer replied.
'Well at least we have somebody with a possible motive, but no connection.' Blake commented. 'I don't want to drag him in for questioning and arouse suspicion at this stage before we have something more concrete, or he might take flight. There's still more groundwork to do. I'd like him put on a twenty four hour surveillance and see what comes to light. I also want the residences of the two culprits watched and a careful record kept of anybody calling round.'
'Sir, we've had a positive ID of the photo.' A young inspector said entering the room. 'It's a Jimmy Warren.' He continued with a smile on his face.
'Well things are really getting hot. Great work, thanks very much.' Blake replied.
'Also Sir, we have a Mary Watts detained at present. She's a young blonde seen entering the first accused house with keys.' An inspector piped up.
'Have we indeed, that sounds intriguing. Bring her into the interview room.' Blake ordered.

Blake entered the interview room to be confronted by leggy heavily made up woman in her late twenties.

'I am Chief Inspector Blake and you are Mary Watts?'

'Yes that's right.' She replied.

'You obviously know Harry Spurgeon because you've been seen entering his house. What is your relationship with him?'

'I'm his girlfriend.'

'I see, and how long have you been his girlfriend?' Blake enquired.

'Must be about eight years now.'

'But you don't live together.'

'No, I've got my own flat, but we stay together occasionally.'

'Do you take drugs Miss. Watts?'

'Yes but only mild ones, mostly at weekends when I'm with Harry.'

'Did you know that Mr. Spurgeon was involved in an attempted murder?'

'No, it was all a bit of a shock for me.'

'Miss Watts, we have obtained a warrant to search your place of residence, in the meantime we are going to detain you.'

'But you won't find any drugs there.'

'Its not drugs we're looking for. Take her down to the cells.' Blake ordered.

So a search of her flat was carried out and underneath her bed they found a briefcase which contained £20,000 in unused £20 notes. When Marry Watts was questioned further she claimed it was payment for a drug deal, but Blake knew she was lying; consequently she was remanded in custody while they continued their inquiries.

After an hours research the police managed to trace where the money had come from, a Midland bank in Islington. Blake and two inspectors paid the bank a visit and they were more than helpful, being able to determine whose account it had been drawn from. Much to Blake's suspicion it was Jimmy Warren's.

So they finally had the correct motive and connection. A full scale search was put out for Jimmy Warren and he was picked up trying to make a departure to India at Heathrow airport. Fortunately, they caught him just in time.

He got a right grilling at the station and ended up admitting to organising the attempted murder, claiming that Dave Potts's theory had completely ruined him.

He received a prison sentence of fifteen years, Mary got eighteen months as an accessory and the other accomplice seven years.

As for Dave Potts, well he won't have to work again, providing things go to plan the new arthritis drug will make him sufficient money to live very comfortably for the rest of his life.

APPENDIX

This appendix outlines the structure of the building industry which the author thought would be useful information for the reader.

The Client
This is the most important person or body of people or organisation and therefore comes at the top of the structure. The client pays for the whole project and decides what he wants with the help of his team.

The Architect
In a traditional contract the client would appoint an architect who would be responsible for designing the building or proposed works and run the job on site issuing instructions to the contractor when necessary, certifying payments on account as work proceeds (these are called valuations and are usually monthly), issuing practical completion certificate when he is satisfied the works are substantially complete, issuing a defects list usually six months after practical completion, then a completion of making good defects certificate once he is satisfied the defects have been completed then a final certificate.

The Quantity Surveyor

The Q.S. is essentially the accountant to the works. He looks after the financial aspects. At pre contract stage he would give an estimate of the proposed works with the information supplied by the architect. If the client decides to go ahead with the works then traditionally the Q.S. would measure all the works from the drawings supplied by the architect, this is called 'taking off', then compile a Bill of Quantities which is essentially a pricing document for the contractor to get the best price for the job which is usually the lowest.

About five or six main contractors are sent the Bill of Quantities for pricing and they are all returned to the Q.S. by a specified time and date. The Q.S. checks the Bill for any arithmetic errors and usually selects the lowest tender unless it is unreasonably low and in their opinion cannot carry out the works for that price, in which case he would encourage the contractor to withdraw his offer because nobody wants a contractor to go bankrupt especially the client as it would be costly engaging another contractor to complete the unfinished works.

When the works are in progress valuations are carried out usually on a monthly basis by the Q.S. who attends site and measures the work and issues a valuation certificate to the architect who authorises a payment on account. If the job was not financed periodically the contractor would have to borrow a lot of money, consequently the client makes a saving by this process.

At the same time as issuing a valuation the Q.S. does a cost report for the client indicating the expected final expenditure. This report is broken down into the various building elements and may contain contingency sums for works which cannot be reasonably evaluated at that stage.

The architect may well require an estimate or quotation from the Q.S. for proposed variations to the works not envisaged at tender stage. The Q.S. would require this information from the contractor. It is a generally accepted thing that the architect does not approach the contractor on financial aspects.

As the works procede sections of the valuations can be used by the Q.S. to compile the final account which is agreed with the contractor after practical completion. Sometimes the Q.S. and contractor do not agree with the cost of some elements of work and the final account is not actually agreed for a considerable length of time.

M&E Consultants

The mechanical and electrical works are specialist and the architect will call on these consultants for the original design and subsequent control of their area of work. They might be asked to advise the architect of suitable subcontractors who might be nominated to carry out the work.

The Main Contractor

This is the organisation that is responsible for carrying out the building work. Over twenty years ago they would directly employ a team of painters and decorators and have their own carpentry workshop, but more recently these works have been subcontracted out to **subcontractors.** At the very least they directly employ site agents responsible for the site, contracts managers, quantity surveyors and estimators who price the work.

Nominated Subcontractors

These subcontractors are nominated to carry out their specialist area of work. Nomination is not favoured these days because they know they've got the job and consequently there is no price control when tendering. They generally have a proven track record or might be recommended to fix a certain product which the architect has put in his design.

Domestic Subcontractors
These days the main contractor will take on domestic subcontractors to carry out the bulk of the work like groundwork, brickwork, roofing, carpentry, labouring and painting and decorating. Very few are directly employed on the cards.

www.ingramcontent.com/pod-product-compliance
Ingram Content Group UK Ltd.
Pitfield, Milton Keynes, MK11 3LW, UK
UKHW041436180426
11947UKWH00007B/468